Happy Birthday, Grampie

Happy Birthday, Grampie

by SUSAN PEARSON
pictures by RONALD HIMLER

Dial Books for Young Readers
· *New York* ·

a pied piper book ®

Published by Dial Books for Young Readers
A Division of Penguin Books USA Inc.
375 Hudson Street · New York, New York 10014

Published simultaneously in Canada by Fitzhenry & Whiteside Limited, Toronto
Text copyright © 1987 by Susan Pearson · Pictures copyright © 1987 by Ronald Himler
All rights reserved
Library of Congress Catalog Card Number: 85-31105
Printed in Hong Kong by South China Printing Company (1988) Limited
First Pied Piper Printing 1990
W
1 3 5 7 9 10 8 6 4 2

A Pied Piper Book is a registered trademark of
Dial Books for Young Readers,
a division of Penguin Books USA Inc.,
® TM 1,163,686 and ® TM 1,054,312.

HAPPY BIRTHDAY, GRAMPIE
is published in a hardcover edition by
Dial Books for Young Readers.
ISBN 0-8037-0779-7

The art consists of watercolor paintings that are color-separated and reproduced in full color.

The author wishes to thank The American Swedish Institute, Minneapolis,
and Monica Stein, Stockholm, for their help.

*In memory of my father
and grandfather* S.P.

*For Nanny and
Pop-Pop Man* R.H.

*M*artha sat at the kitchen table, working. The sun beat through the checkered curtains, and she could hear Mommy humming and water running in the bathroom. It was almost time to get ready.

She was just about finished, but Martha didn't want to hurry. Sticking the letters onto the felt was the trickiest part. *Happy Birthday, Grampie. I Love You.*

There. She was done. She held the card up, pleased with her work. This was one card Grampie would be able to "see" even though he was blind, because Martha had made it in a special way. Every part of it had a different feeling — the construction paper on the bottom, then the paper doily, then the piece of felt cut like a heart, and finally, the shiny, stick-on letters. She touched her finger to each letter, tracing it. She wanted Grampie to "read" it too.

Martha got dressed, then read the funnies with Daddy until the bells began to ring. They started at exactly nine-thirty every Sunday morning, and they meant that it was time to go to church. Martha and Mommy and Daddy always walked, no matter what the weather. Today was hot, but Martha knew that inside the church it would be cool and a little damp — like just after a rainstorm, she thought.

There were a lot of things Martha liked about going to church: the way everyone whispered hello, the colored puddles made by the sun shining through the stained glass windows, the singing, putting her own envelope in the collection plate. She did not like the hard wooden pews or the minister talking, but this morning they didn't bother her because she was thinking about Grampie.

Martha's family visited Grampie every Sunday, but this Sunday was special. Grampie was eighty-nine years old this very day. In other years his birthday had really been on Tuesday or Wednesday, and they had just pretended that it was on Sunday. But this year it *was* on Sunday.

Every time they visited, Grampie gave Martha one dollar. Part of it she put into her bank. Part of it she spent. And lately part of it she put into a cigar box in her top bureau drawer — Grampie's Birthday Box. Yesterday she had taken the money from the box and gone shopping with Daddy for Grampie's birthday present: a tin of his favorite tobacco. They'd had to go to a special store to find it because it was Swedish tobacco.

As soon as they got home from church, they left for Auburn, where Grampie lived. The drive took about two hours, and Martha spent the time picking out her favorite houses or imagining that she was on a horse in a race with their car. On the way they passed Aunt Margaret and Uncle Tom's house. They used to go there for Sunday dinner sometimes when Grampie had been able to come along. Martha remembered Grampie pushing her on the tree swing in their backyard. He'd been old then, too, she supposed, but he'd been bigger and fatter, she thought, and he'd laughed a lot. He'd had a great big laugh that used to make Martha laugh too. That was before his hands shook, when he could still see. It was a long time ago.

As they got closer, Mommy began to sing, and Martha and Daddy joined in. First, "I've Been Workin' on the Railroad," then "Goober Peas." This morning the singing reminded Martha of the time she'd sung "Twinkle, Twinkle, Little Star" in Swedish for Grampie. It was called *"Blinka Lilla Stjärna"* and she'd learned it especially for him. Grampie had clapped, and he'd even sung with her the second time around. He didn't speak English anymore by then, just Swedish, but Martha could remember a time when he had spoken English. Sometimes he'd forgotten a few of the words, so he'd said them in Swedish, but now he didn't seem to remember any English words at all. Daddy said Grampie had grown up in Sweden and hadn't learned English until he'd come to the United States. He said that sometimes when people got very old they could only remember the first language they'd learned.

Martha still knew the words to *"Blinka Lilla Stjärna"* but that was all the Swedish she knew except for *tack så mycket*. That meant "thank you," and she said it every week when Grampie gave her the crisp new dollar bill. And *var så god*. That meant "you're welcome," and it was what Grampie said to her. She hoped Grampie would remember enough English to read "Happy Birthday, Grampie. I Love You."

Grampie lived in a big house on a quiet street with some other old people and a lot of nurses. Whenever they went to see him, he was in his bedroom, but Martha didn't mind because the room was big and sunny.

One of the nurses, Mrs. Carlson, met them at the door. "Hello," she said. "It's nice to see you again."

Mrs. Carlson always took them upstairs to Grampie's room as if they didn't know where they were going. She said something to Grampie in Swedish — probably exactly the same thing she always said, Martha thought — then left, closing the door quietly behind her. Daddy sat down next to Grampie, Mommy sat in a chair across the room, and Martha sat on the window ledge. For a long time Daddy and Grampie talked to each other in Swedish. Martha wondered what they were saying; it sounded so pretty. Sometimes at home she would ask Daddy to talk to *her* in Swedish. Today their talk was like a lullaby, and Martha almost fell asleep.

All of a sudden the door opened. The nurses were standing in the doorway, and Mrs. Carlson was holding a big birthday cake. They all sang "Happy Birthday," and when they came to the part where you put in the name, everyone except Daddy and Martha sang "Happy birthday, dear August." Martha sang "Grampie," and Daddy sang "Papa," which sounded funny to Martha. Grampie looked surprised, as if he had forgotten that it was his birthday. He grinned in an embarrassed kind of way.

Daddy helped Grampie cut the first piece of cake, then he cut the rest. There was ice cream, too, and then the presents. A new pipe, some after-shave lotion, a new bathrobe, a pair of slippers, and finally it was Martha's turn.

"Here, Grampie," she said softly.

Grampie unwrapped the tobacco. He felt the tin can. Daddy said something to him in Swedish, and Grampie smiled. He reached out his hand and felt for Martha's head like he always did. He put his hand on top of her head, and Martha could feel it shaking.

"*Tack så mycket*," he said.

"*Var så god*," Martha answered. This was the first time she'd ever said "you're welcome" in Swedish.

Then Martha handed him the card. She held her breath. Grampie felt the construction paper. Then his fingers explored the doily. He touched the felt heart. And at last his fingers were tracing over the letters. Daddy didn't tell him anything in Swedish; Martha had made him promise. Everyone was quiet, watching Grampie concentrate on the letters.

And then Grampie's face seemed to light up, his smile got bigger, and he laughed a big laugh — the kind that made Martha, and everyone else, laugh with him. He reached out his hand to find Martha, and when he did, he pulled her close and gave her a big bear hug and Martha didn't feel his arms shaking even a little.

He whispered something in Swedish that made Daddy smile.

And then, out loud, he said in English, "Martha, I love you, too."

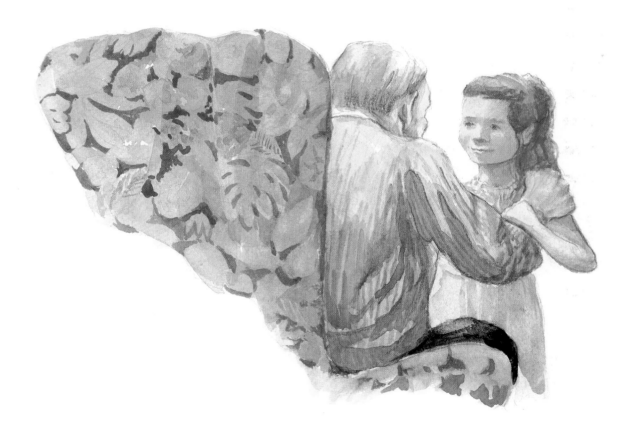